Mr. Blewitt's NOSE

featuring **Primrose Pumpkin,**

her **Helpful Nature**

& her Incredibly Smelly Dog, **Dirk**

written & illustrated by **Alastair Taylor**

Houghton Mifflin Company Boston 2005

For Catherine Lillycrop, who helped

www.houghtonmifflinbooks.com

The text of this book is set in 17.5-point Graham Bold.
The illustrations are acrylics.

Library of Congress Cataloging-in-Publication Data
Taylor, Alastair.
Mr. Blewitt's nose / by Alastair Taylor.
p. cm.
Summary: Primrose Pumpkin, who always tries to be helpful, and her dog Dirk,
who is very smelly, try to locate the owner of a nose they find on a park bench.
ISBN 0-618-42353-2
[1. Smell—Fiction. 2. Dogs—Fiction. 3. Nose—Fiction.
4. Senses and sensation—Fiction.] I. Title.
PZ7.T211577Mr 2005   [E]—dc22   2004013413

ISBN 13: 978-0618-42353-8

Printed in Singapore
TWP 10 9 8 7 6 5 4 3 2 1

Primrose Pumpkin had a helpful nature

and an outrageously smelly dog, **Dirk**.

Primrose Pumpkin was so used to Dirk's remarkable stinkiness that she could quite happily take him for walks and hardly notice it.

Other people, though, would cross to the other side of the street as they approached to get away from the dreadful smell.

The sidewalk was never crowded when Primrose Pumpkin took her alarmingly smelly dog, Dirk, for a walk.

It was on one such walk that she noticed something very unusual, something you rarely see on an average street in a normal town on a humdrum sort of day. At least, not on its own.

It was a nose.

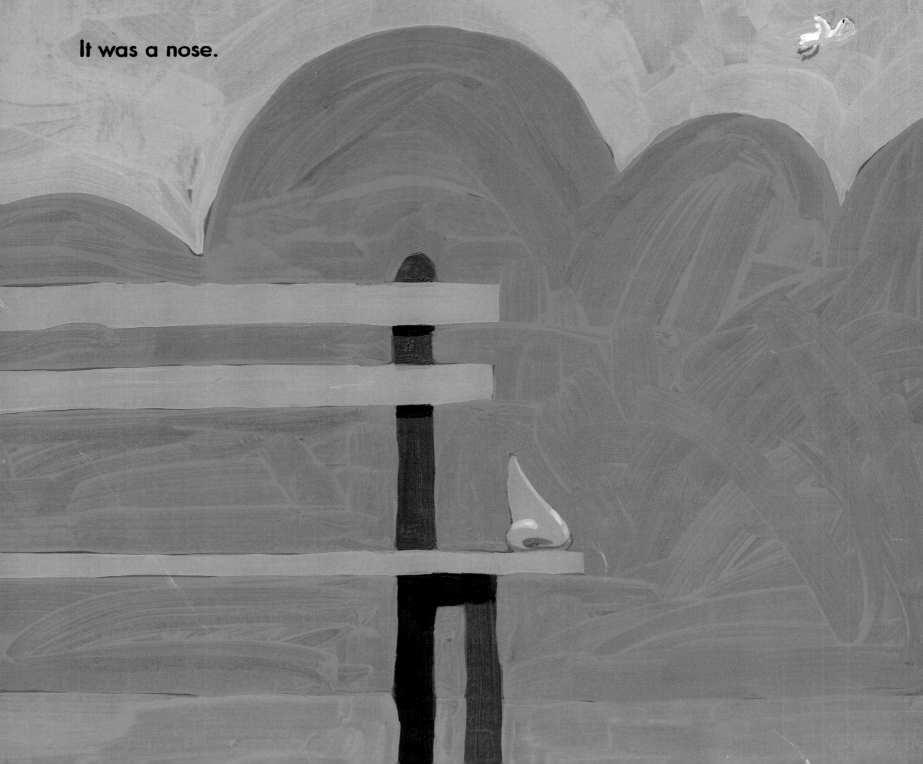

It was perched on the end of a park bench, as if someone had removed it for a moment and then forgotten and gone off without it. No one else seemed to have noticed it (and no one was likely to as long as Primrose Pumpkin's outstandingly smelly dog, Dirk, was anywhere near).

Primrose Pumpkin concluded that if there was a nose without a person attached, then it followed that somewhere there was a person without a nose attached. And, as she had a helpful nature, she decided to find that person.

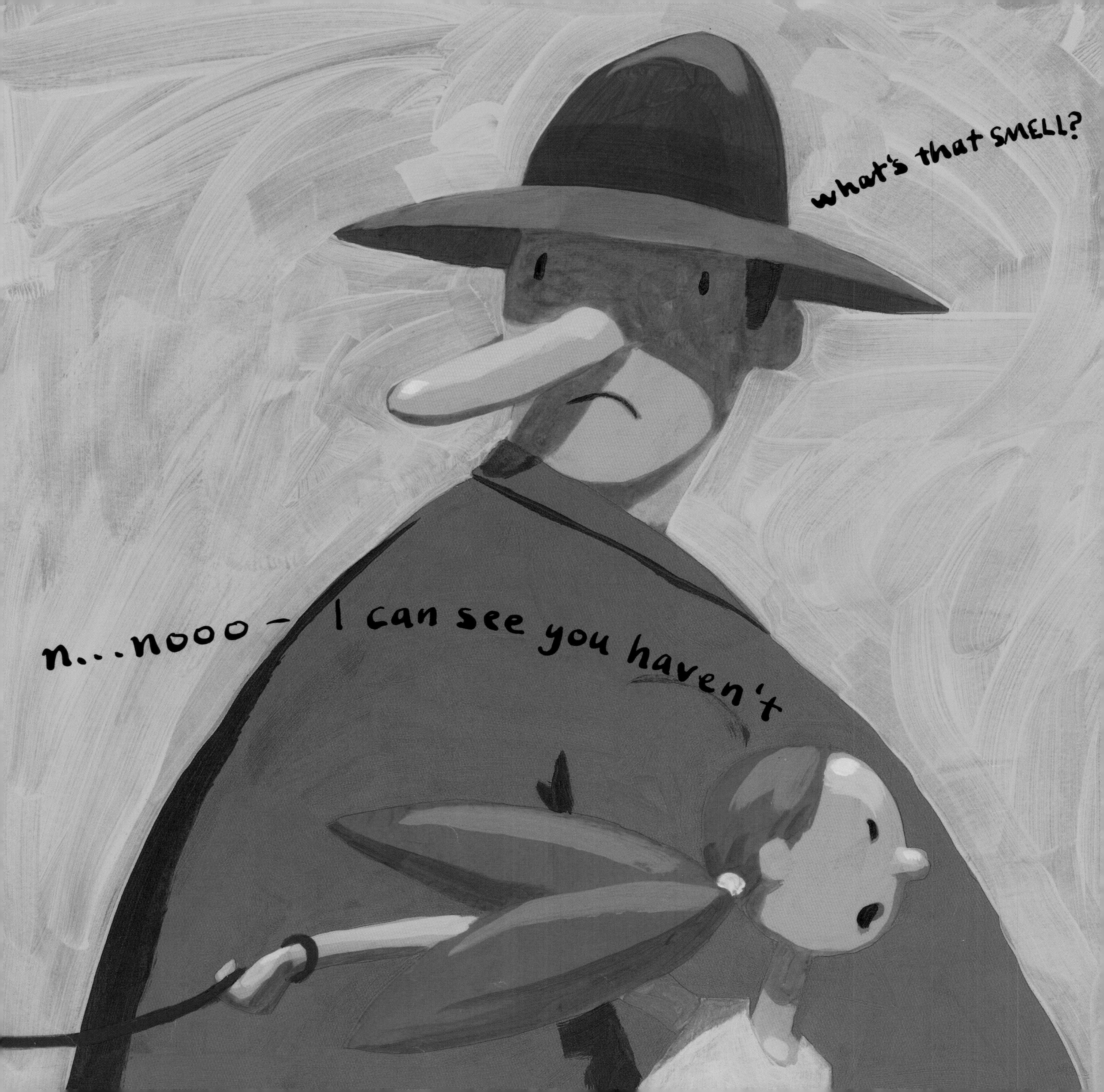
what's that SMELL?
n...nooo—
I can see you haven't

anybody lost a NOSE ?

Primrose Pumpkin soon realized that there wasn't much point in asking people who obviously had noses whether they had lost theirs. It was more a case of asking if they might know of anyone who could possibly have lost a nose. But this took just a little longer to ask, longer than most people could put up with the odor emanating from her sensationally smelly dog, Dirk.

Primrose Pumpkin was beginning to wonder if it was worth all the trouble.
But her helpful nature prevailed, and she tried a new way of
advertising the problem.

IF YOU HAVE LOST YOUR
N O S E
it's here

And sure enough . . .

OK, this is as close as I get . . .
That there nose'll belong to
MR. BLEWITT. He's ALWAYS
leaving it around the place.
'Bout this time he'll be going
to watch the game.
Always wears a red shirt.
Right, it's getting stinky — I'm off.

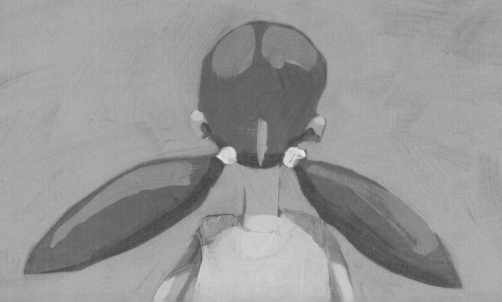

She hadn't gone far in the direction pointed when she spotted in the distance a man in a red shirt.

She hurried after him, dragging her inconceivably smelly dog, Dirk, behind her.

But as she rounded a corner, Primrose Pumpkin crashed into ANOTHER man in a red shirt; a man obviously in full possession of his nose . . . He started to help her up, but soon thought better of it.

By now there were dozens, maybe even hundreds, of people in red shirts all heading in the same direction. Primrose Pumpkin asked a woman with a bad cold what was going on.

there's a gabe od today at the stadiub—
red's the hobe teab's color

(And even she could detect a bit
of a nasty whiff.)

Still not knowing how she was going to spot Mr. Blewitt among the mass of red-shirted people, Primrose Pumpkin joined the crowd going into the stadium. She didn't even have to pay, as the ticket man turned a very odd color and fell off his stool as she and the outlandishly smelly dog, Dirk, approached.

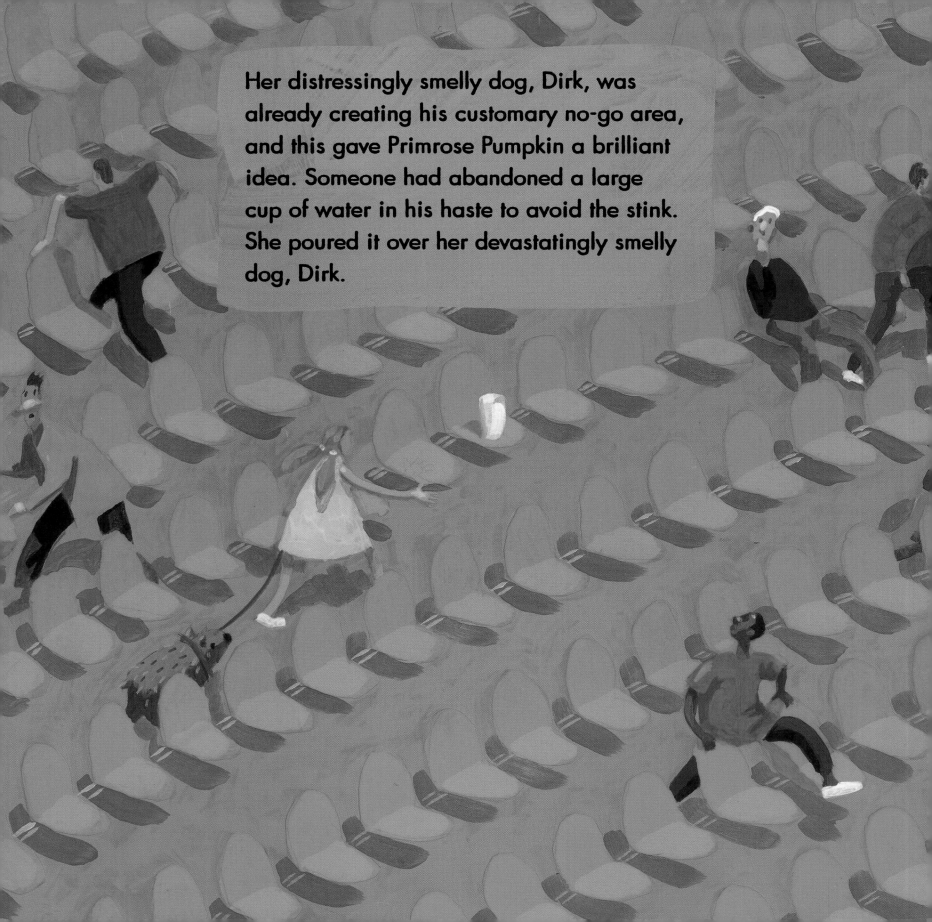

Her distressingly smelly dog, Dirk, was already creating his customary no-go area, and this gave Primrose Pumpkin a brilliant idea. Someone had abandoned a large cup of water in his haste to avoid the stink. She poured it over her devastatingly smelly dog, Dirk.

If Dirk was smelly when he was dry, there are no words to describe how smelly he was when wet. Even Primrose Pumpkin herself felt a little queasy, and she was used to him. To almost everyone else in the stadium there was only one thing to do, and they all did it.

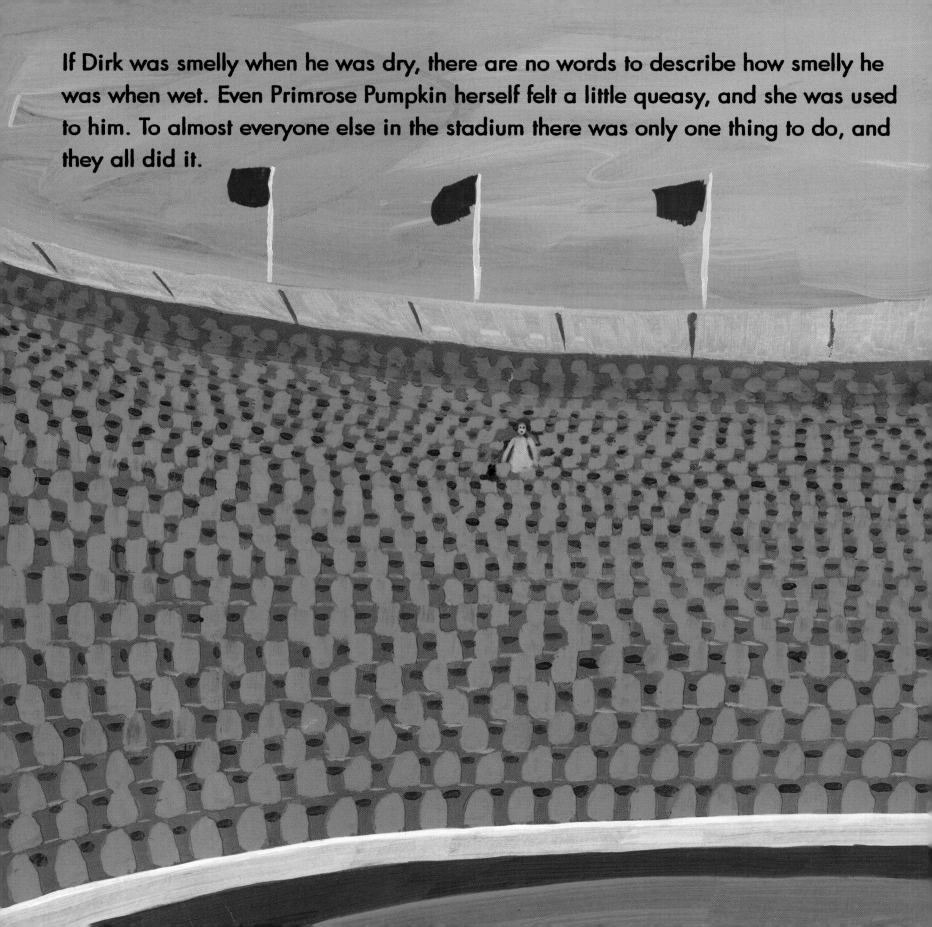

In minutes the stadium was empty except for Primrose Pumpkin . . .

her eye-wateringly smelly dog, Dirk . . .

and Mr. Blewitt.

Mr. Blewitt was having a perplexing day. First he had gone and mislaid his nose somehow. Then he couldn't understand why as soon as he arrived at the stadium to watch the game, everyone else left. And now here was a little girl he had never seen before, with an unsavory-looking dog in tow, addressing him by name!

MR. BLEWITT!

Mr. Blewitt replaced his nose and, as you might expect, it fitted him perfectly. He was delighted.

The next morning Primrose Pumpkin received a bunch of sweet-scented flowers and an invitation to tea with Mr. Blewitt. There was no mention on the invitation card of Dirk.